Sharon Morris

Illustrations by Devon Morris

The Atlas of Alliterative Animal Adventures

Bumblebee Books
London

BUMBLEBEE PAPERBACK EDITION

Copyright © Sharon Morris 2022
Illustrations by Devon Morris

The right of Sharon Morris to be identified as author of
this work has been asserted in accordance with sections 77 and 78 of the Copyright, Designs and Patents Act 1988.

A CIP catalogue record for this title is
available from the British Library.

ISBN: 978-1-83934-555-5

Bumblebee Books is an imprint of
Olympia Publishers.

First Published in 2022

Bumblebee Books
Tallis House
2 Tallis Street
London
EC4Y 0AB

Printed in Great Britain

www.olympiapublishers.com

Dedication

I dedicate this book to my children and my grandchildren.

Ally the ambitious aardvark athletically accomplishes aerial acrobatics in an airplane alongside the adorable alpaca above the ancient Andes.

Breno the bowlegged baboon boldly bangs his big bright bongos by the bonny beach in Brazil.

Carlos the colorful cuttle-fish cheerfully captivates the crowd of crocodiles while calmly conducting a classical concert in C minor, with calico cats in Cuba.

Devon the dapper donkey, dressed in a dinner jacket, delightfully dines on dozens of delicious daffodils while in the deserts of Dubai.

Elliot the eccentric elephant excitedly educates eleven exotic emus about the environment of Egypt.

Francisco the fearless frog fiercely fences five frantic flamingoes at the fountains in Florence.

Garrett the grungy gray goat gleefully gobbles garbage while a gathering of gracious gazelles gasp at his gluttony on the Ganges.

Harry the hipster hippo happily hitchhikes to the hip-hop happening at the Hong Kong harbor.

Imogeen the ice-skating iguana intensely investigates the indigo inchworm's intimate ice-cream social along the ice-caps of Iceland.

James the jovial jaguar jauntily jiggles in his jeep while journeying through the jungles of Java, jeopardizing his jars of jam.

Kaelen the kimonoed koala has a knack for cooking kimchee in her kitchen in Korea.

Luca and Louis the lanky lobsters lick lemon-lime lollipops while lazily log rolling in the lagoons of Louisiana.

Milo the mighty mystical manta ray meanders magnificently amongst the marine milieu in the Maldives.

Ned the nearsighted nautical newt nimbly navigates the narrows of Norway while noisily nibbling a non-nutritious napoleon.

Ollie the opulent octopus often orders oily olives and organic oranges in an oasis in Oman.

Peter the powerful peacock proudly pole vaults over a paddock of ponies in the picturesque pampas of Paraguay.

Quinn the quirky quail quizzically quests for quality quilts in the quaint quarters of Quebec.

Ryan the rascally raccoon recklessly rappels the rickety rafters of the ramshackle ruins in Romania.

Seymore the swashbuckling shark swiftly saves Sal the sizeable snail in the shimmering seas surrounding Singapore.

Tadeo the towering T-Rex tenaciously teaches Taekwondo to a teeny-tiny tortoise in tropical Tobago.

Uzoma the understanding uakari up-liftingly utilizes their ukulele to unite unicycling unicorns at the University of Uganda.

Vinnie the vegetarian vulture voraciously vanishes vats of Vegemite while vacationing in vibrant Vietnam.

Winnie the whistling walrus wildly weaves their wakeboard on the wicked waves of Wollongong.

Xavier the exacting xenurine exhaustingly xeriscapes xeranthemums in X'ian.

Yolanda the youthful yellow-beaded yak yearly yerns for yoga in Yosemite.

Ziggy the zany zebra zestfully zig zags on his Zamboni across the Zanzibar Zoo.

About the Author

Sharon Morris was an elementary school teacher, who taught in Singapore for many years. She enjoyed working with children who were just exploring the English language and loved to see how quickly they could learn. Sharon now lives in Bellingham Washington, with her husband Steve, their two dogs and fourteen chickens.

Acknowledgements

Thank you to Steve for encouraging me to finish my book and for helping me create some of the sillier alliterations!

Thank you Devon for your fantastic illustrations – I knew you could do it!

Wheels

Alan Truswell-Cullen

Nelson Thornes

Nelson Thornes

First published in 2007 by Cengage Learning Australia
www.cengage.com.au

This edition published in 2008 under the imprint of Nelson Thornes Ltd,
Delta Place, 27 Bath Road, Cheltenham, United Kingdom, GL53 7TH

10 9 8 7 6 5 4 3 2
11 10 09 08

Wheels
ISBN 978-1-4085-0122-1

Text by Alan Trussell-Cullen
Edited by Cameron Macintosh
Designed by James Lowe
Series Design by James Lowe
Production Controller Seona Galbally
Photo Research by Gillian Cardinal
Audio recordings by Juliet Hill, Picture Start
Spoken by Matthew King and Abbe Holmes
Printed in China by 1010 Printing International Ltd

Website www.nelsonthornes.com

Acknowledgements
The author and publisher would like to acknowledge permission to reproduce material from
the following sources:
Photographs by AAP Image/Jose Jordan, pp. 3, 19 /Franck Fife, p. 12 /Giuseppe Cacace, p. 13 /4X4 Australia,
p. 16 /Dean Lewis, p. 17 /Matt Campbell, p. 20; Almay/Ukraft, p. 18; APL/Corbis/Stepleton Collection, p. 6 /
Underwood & Underwood, p. 7 bottom /Historical Picture Archive, p. 10 /Sean Sexton Collection, p. 11;
Getty Images/The Image Bank/ Mark S Wexler, front cover, p. 21 /Taxi/Mike Owen, p. 8 /The Image Bank/
Angelo Cavalli, back cover, p. 15; Mary Evans Picture Library, p. 5 top; Masterfile/R. Ian Lloyd, p. 22 /Andrew
Wenzel, p. 23; Photolibrary.com/Creatas, p.7 top /John Arnold Images/John Coletti, p. 9 top /The Bridgemen
Art Library, p. 9 bottom /Alamy/David Young-Wolff, p. 14; The Art Archive/Bibliothéque des Arts Déscoratifs
Paris/Dagli Orti, p. 5 bottom.

Wheels

Alan Trussell-Cullen

Contents

Chapter 1   History of the Wheel   4

Chapter 2   One Wheel   8

Chapter 3   Two Wheels   10

Chapter 4   Three Wheels   14

Chapter 5   Four Wheels   16

Chapter 6   Lots of Wheels   22

Glossary and Index   24

HISTORY OF THE WHEEL

It is believed that the wheel was invented in **Mesopotamia** in about 3500 BC.

Early wheels were wooden disks with a hole for an **axle**. They were used as potters' wheels.

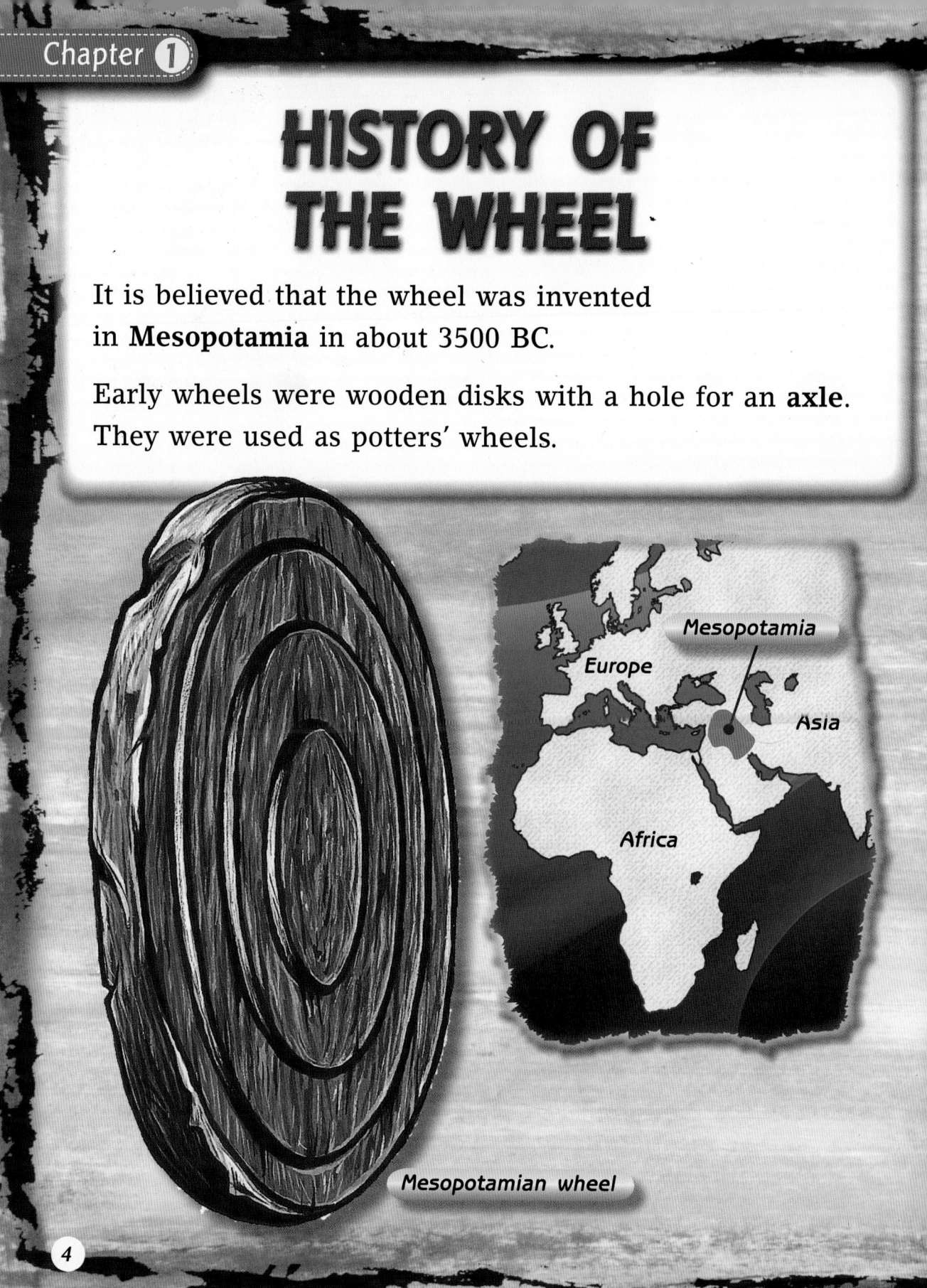

Mesopotamian wheel

In about 3200 BC,
the wheel was first used
for transport.
It was used on
Mesopotamian chariots.
The wheels were heavy
and travel was slow.

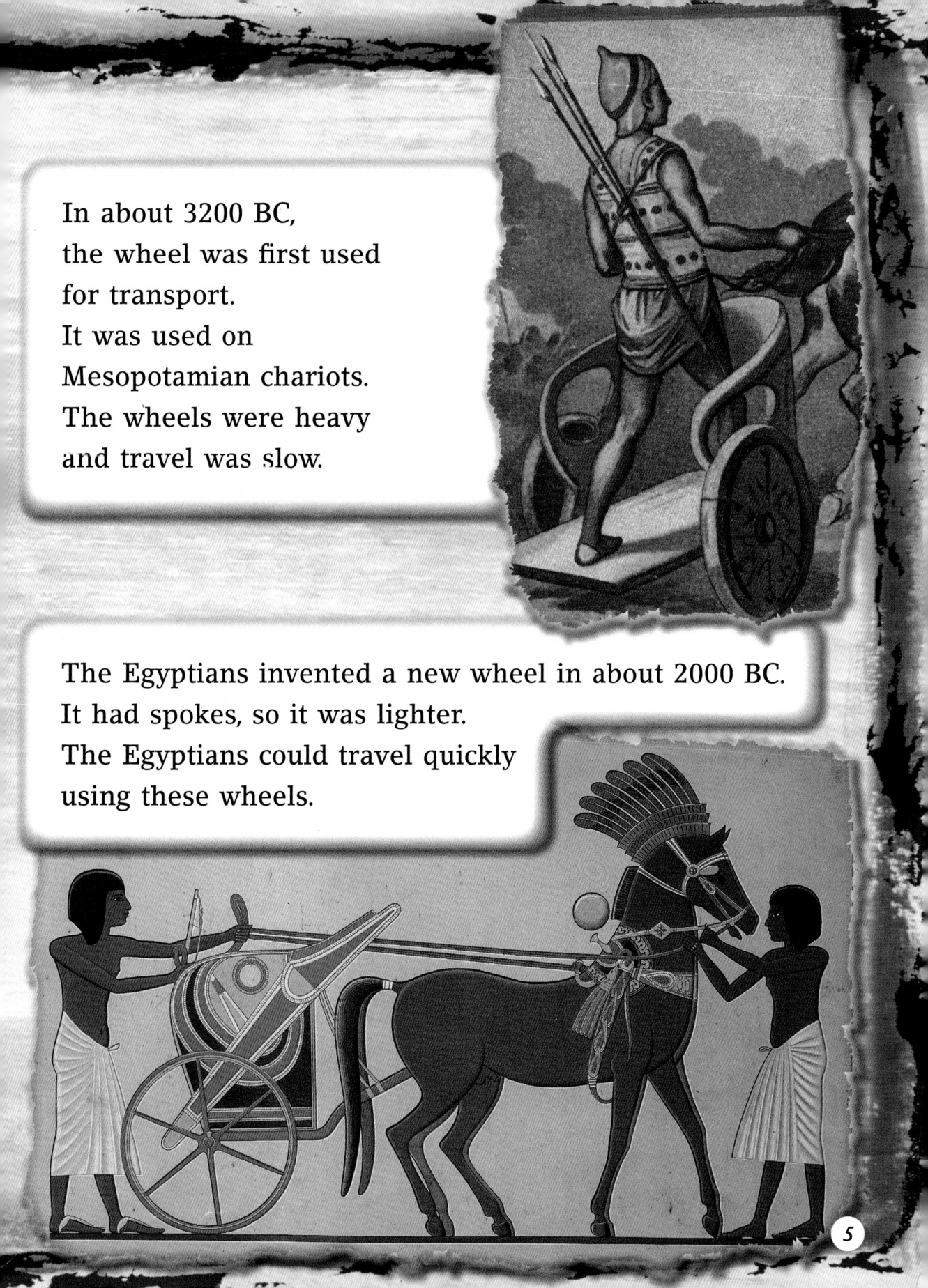

The Egyptians invented a new wheel in about 2000 BC.
It had spokes, so it was lighter.
The Egyptians could travel quickly
using these wheels.

The **Romans** used wheels with spokes
on their chariots, too.
They also made roads so they could travel quickly
from one place to another.

The wheel didn't change a lot
until the nineteenth century.
At that time, people started putting
metal tyres on wheels
to make them last longer.

Henry Ford in his first car

metal tyre

rubber tyres

In 1888, metal tyres were replaced
with rubber tyres, filled with air.
These tyres gave people
a much more comfortable ride.

Running Words 152

7

Chapter 2

ONE WHEEL

Forms of transport are classified by
the number of wheels they have.
Some forms of transport have one wheel.

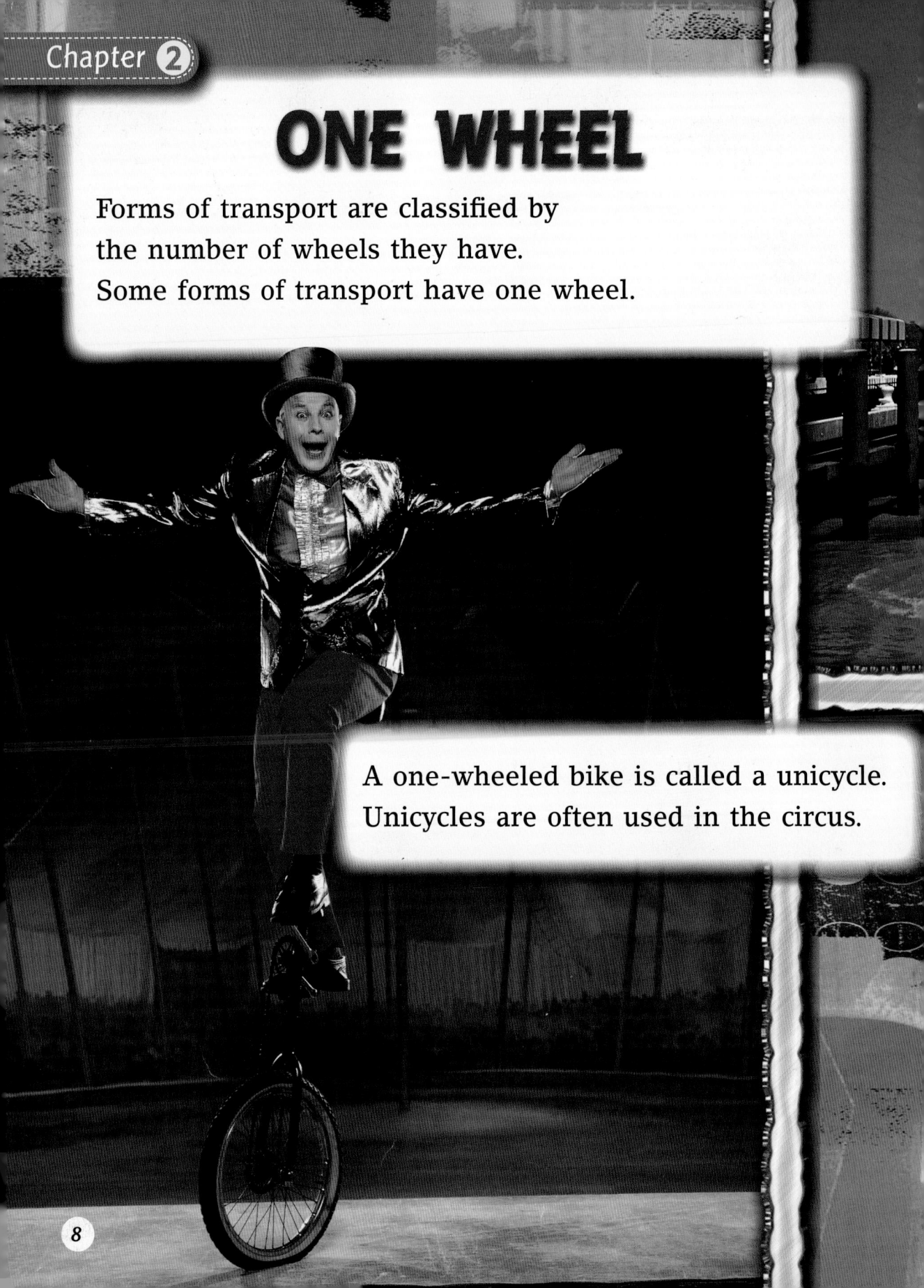

A one-wheeled bike is called a unicycle.
Unicycles are often used in the circus.

The paddle steamer has one wheel.
It has paddles on a big wheel
that push it along in the water
as the wheel turns.

Wheel Fact

The Ferris Wheel
is one very large wheel.
It was invented by George Ferris in 1893.
The first Ferris Wheel was very big –
it was 26 storeys high,
and could take 2160 people
at a time!

Chapter 3

TWO WHEELS

Some forms of transport have two wheels.

Bicycles have two wheels.
The first bicycle had no pedals,
so the rider pushed it along with his or her feet.

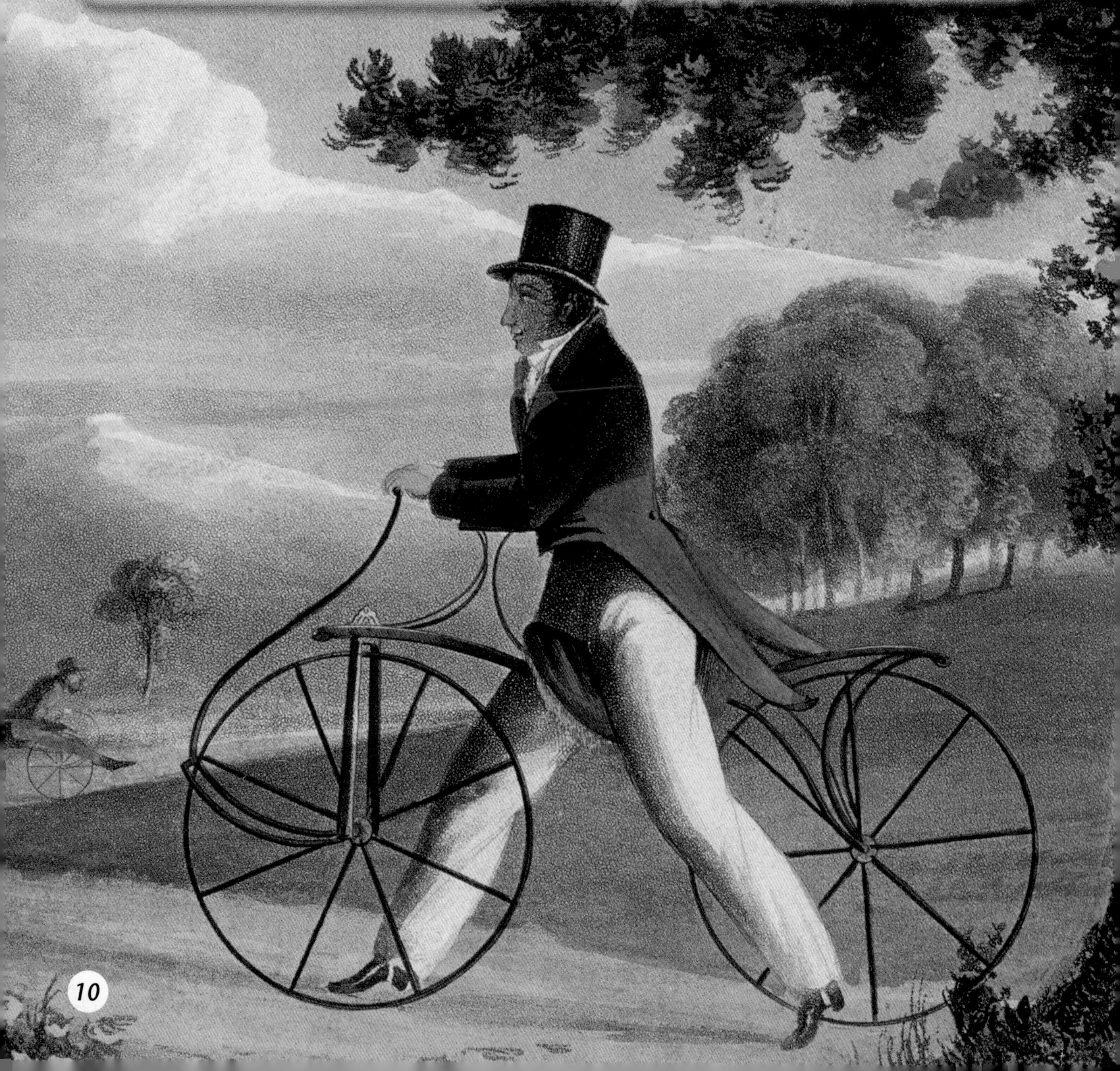

Another early bicycle was the penny-farthing.
It had pedals, and could go quite fast.
The penny-farthing was named after two coins –
a big one (the penny) and a small one (the farthing).

Today, there are many kinds of bicycles.
Each kind of bicycle has different tyres,
depending on what the bicycle is used for.
Bicycles for riding on roads
have thin tyres.

Bicycles for riding on rocky, uneven ground have thick tyres.

Chapter 4

THREE WHEELS

Some forms of transport have three wheels.

Tricycles have three wheels.
They are easier to ride than bicycles
because the three wheels help the rider to balance.

A cycle rickshaw also has three wheels.
It is used to carry passengers.
The driver sits in front of the passengers
and pedals them from place to place.

Chapter 5

FOUR WHEELS

Some forms of transport have four wheels.

Cars have four wheels.
A car uses a motor to drive the wheels.

Car wheels are protected by tyres.
Today, tyres are made to help cars
drive safely in all weather conditions
and on different kinds of ground.

Formula One cars travel very fast.
The tyres of a Formula One car have four grooves.
These grooves help to keep the car's speed under control when it goes around corners.

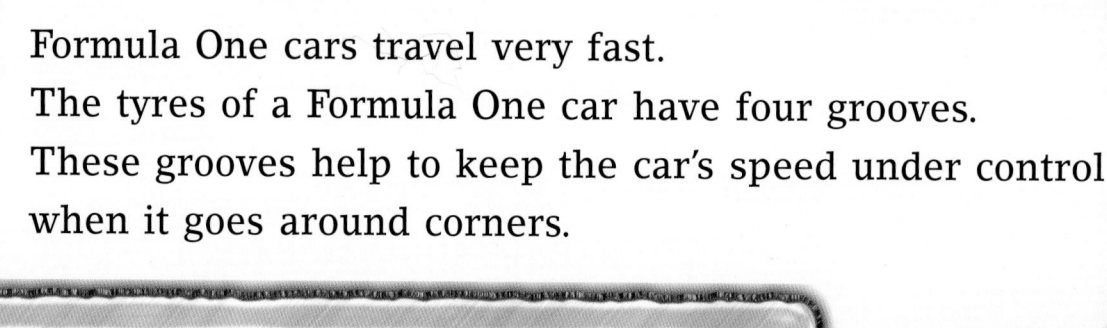

The back wheels are wider than the front wheels. This also helps to control the car's speed.

Monster trucks have four wheels.
They are used to crush big things like cars,
so their wheels are huge.

The tyres on the wheels are very thick.
These large tyres help to protect
the monster truck and the driver
as the truck crushes the things in its way.

Chapter 6

LOTS OF WHEELS

Some forms of transport have lots of wheels.
Trains have lots of wheels.
The wheels on a train are made from steel,
not rubber like a car's wheels.
Trains need steel wheels because they travel so far,
and steel wheels don't wear out like rubber tyres.

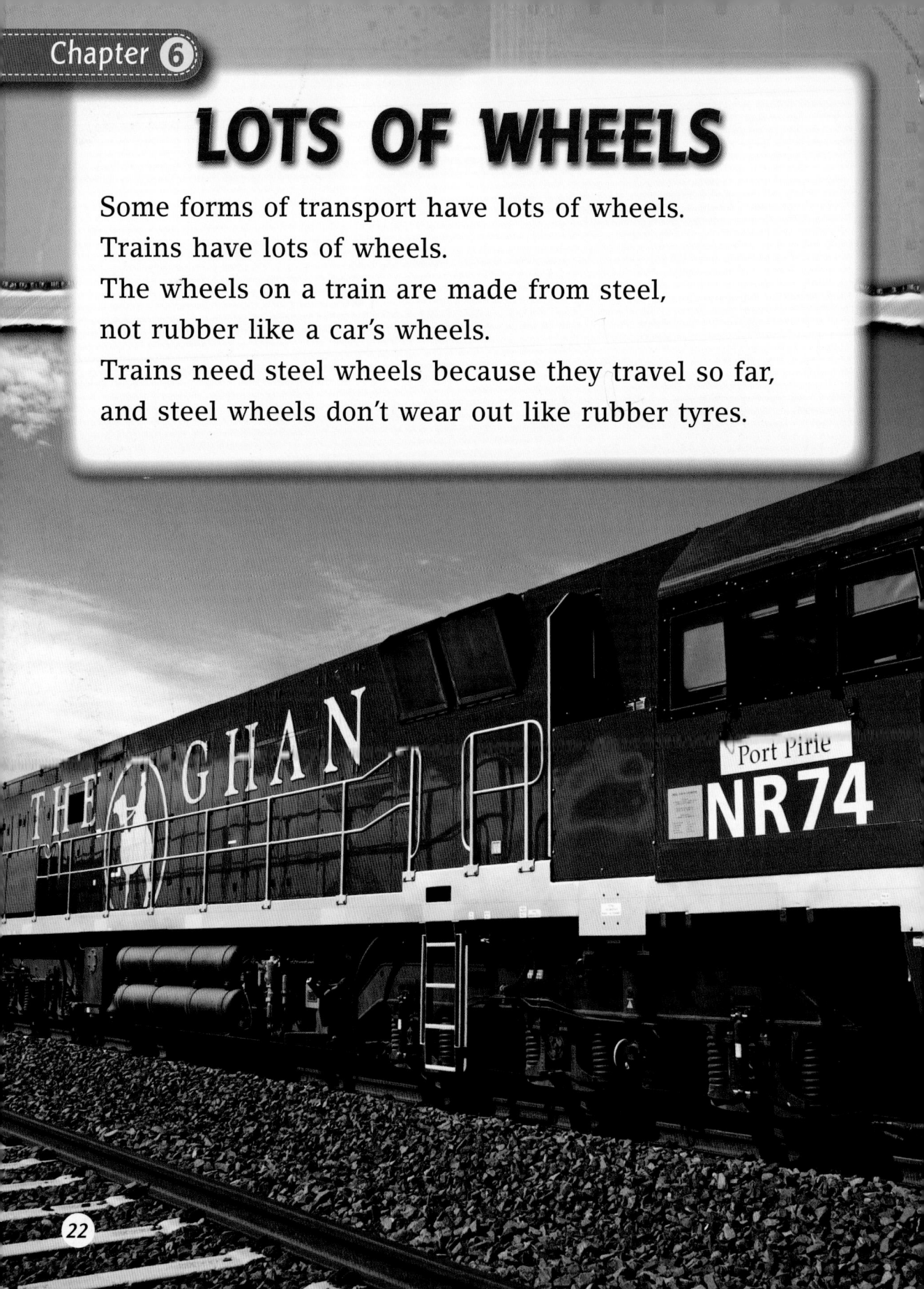

Unlike rubber tyres, steel wheels keep their shape over time and distance.

Glossary

axle	a shaft on which a wheel rotates
chariots	two-wheeled vehicles, drawn by horses
Mesopotamia	an ancient empire, that once ruled over a large part of modern-day Iraq
Romans	people who lived in ancient Rome, during the period of 27 BC to AD 476

Index

axle   4

bicycle   10–13, 14

cars   7, 16–19, 20, 22

chariot   5, 6

Egyptians   5

Ferris Wheel   9

Formula One   18–19

Mesopotamia   4, 5

monster trucks   20–21

paddle steamer   9

penny-farthing   11

rickshaw   15

Romans   6

spokes   5, 6

trains   22–23

transport   8, 10, 14, 16, 22

tricycle   14

tyres   7, 12, 13, 17, 18, 21, 22, 23

unicycle   8